Katie Kazoo, SWITCHEROO

Red, White, and—Achoo!

by Nancy Krulik • illustrated by John & Wendy

Grosset & Dunlap
An Imprint of Penguin Group (USA) Inc.

For Mandy and Ian, who make every day a
celebration (or *almost* every day, anyway!)—N.K.

To a Little Girl, who doesn't like sneezes.—J&W

GROSSET & DUNLAP
Published by the Penguin Group
Penguin Group (USA) Inc., 375 Hudson Street, New York,
New York 10014, USA
Penguin Group (Canada), 90 Eglinton Avenue East, Suite 700, Toronto,
Ontario M4P 2Y3, Canada
(a division of Pearson Penguin Canada Inc.)
Penguin Books Ltd., 80 Strand, London WC2R 0RL, England
Penguin Group Ireland, 25 St. Stephen's Green, Dublin 2,
Ireland(a division of Penguin Books Ltd.)
Penguin Group (Australia), 250 Camberwell Road, Camberwell, Victoria 3124,
Australia(a division of Pearson Australia Group Pty. Ltd.)
Penguin Books India Pvt. Ltd., 11 Community Centre, Panchsheel Park,
New Delhi—110 017, India
Penguin Group (NZ), 67 Apollo Drive, Rosedale, North Shore 0632,
New Zealand (a division of Pearson New Zealand Ltd.)
Penguin Books (South Africa) (Pty.) Ltd., 24 Sturdee Avenue,
Rosebank, Johannesburg 2196, South Africa

Penguin Books Ltd., Registered Offices:
80 Strand, London WC2R 0RL, England

Library of Congress Control Number: 2009015678

ISBN 978-0-448-45230-2   10 9 8 7 6 5 4 3 2 1

Chapter 1

"Achoo!" Katie Carew sneezed as she picked up her ringing telephone. "Huddo?"

"Hello," the voice on the other end said. "And gesundheit."

"Dank you, Emma," Katie said to her friend, Emma Weber. "How was school today?"

"Just a regular day," Emma told Katie. "Mr. Guthrie dressed up like President Teddy Roosevelt. He carried around a teddy bear."

Katie smiled. That *did* sound like a typical school day—at least in class 4A. Her teacher was always dressing up in funny costumes. Presidents' Day was coming up soon. That's why Mr. G. must have dressed up like President Roosevelt.

"Mr. G. told us the teddy bear was named after Teddy Roosevelt," Emma told Katie. "I had no idea."

Katie was about to say, "Me neither." Instead she let out another sneeze.

"Gesundheit again," Emma said. "I guess your cold isn't getting any better."

"It is, a little," Katie told her. My mom says if I rest all weekend, I can probably go to school on Monday."

"That's awesome!" Emma exclaimed. "School's not as much fun without you."

"Danks," Katie said. She blew her stuffy nose. "Do we have any homework?"

"No," Emma told her. "Next week we'll be researching stuff for our Presidents' Day learning adventure."

Mr. G. thought school should be an adventure, so he called each new unit a learning adventure.

"Do we get to pick which president we want to learn about?" Katie asked excitedly. Doing a report on President Obama would be really fun.

"No," Emma said. "Mr. G. pulled names from a hat. Your president is Millard Fillmore."

"Who?" Katie asked.

"Millard Fillmore."

"I've never heard of him," Katie said disappointedly. "Who did you get?"

"Thomas Jefferson," Emma said. "He wrote the Declaration of Independence. Ms. Folio helped me find some information about him in the library today."

"You're lucky," Katie said. "You got a good president. I got some guy no one's heard of."

"I'm sorry," Emma said.

"It's not your fault," Katie said. Then she sneezed again. "I'm not feeling so well. Maybe I should hang up now."

"Okay," Emma said. "I hope you feel better."

As she hung up with Emma, Katie coughed hard. Then she sighed. "Millard Fillmore. That really stinks. I wi—"

Katie stopped herself. She'd almost made a wish. That would have been a big mistake. Katie knew first hand that the only thing worse than having a really stuffy nose, being stuck inside for a whole weekend, and having to do a project about Millard Fillmore, would be having a wish come true.

After all, wishes could be dangerous things.

Chapter 2

It had all started one horrible day back in third grade. First, Katie had missed the football and lost the game for her team. Then she'd fallen in the mud and ruined her new jeans. Worst of all, she'd let out a giant burp right in front of the whole class. The kids had really teased her about that. Especially George Brennan. And he could be a really bad teaser.

It had definitely been one of the most embarrassing days of Katie's whole life. And that night, Katie wished she could be anyone but herself. There must have been a shooting star flying overhead when Katie made her wish, because the very next day the magic wind came.

The magic wind was unlike any wind Katie had ever seen before. It was a wild, fierce tornado that only blew around Katie.

But the worst part came after the wind *stopped* blowing. That's when the magic wind turned Katie into someone else. One . . . two . . . switcheroo!

The magic wind could turn Katie into anyone. The first time it appeared, it changed her into Speedy, the hamster in her third-grade classroom. Katie spent the whole morning going around and around on a hamster wheel, and chewing on Speedy's wooden chew sticks. *Blech!* They tasted worse than the food in the school cafeteria!

The magic wind had come back many times after that. One time it turned her into her own mom—right in the middle of a big tap dancing competition. Katie's feet got all twisted up, and she fell smack on her rear end. That had been really embarrassing, especially for Katie's mom.

That was the biggest problem with the magic wind. Whoever it turned her into wound up smack in the middle of a real mess. And when the wind switcherooed Katie back into herself, it was up to her to figure out how to clean that mess up!

That was why Katie didn't make wishes any more. They caused too much trouble.

Rrring. Rrring. It was the phone again.

"Heddo," Katie said.

This time it was her best friend, Suzanne. "Boy, you sound awful, Katie," Suzanne said.

"I just have a stuffed-up nose," Katie explained. "But I'm getting better. It was really nice of you to call to check on how I'm feeling."

"Oh, yeah, you were absent today. I forgot," Suzanne said.

"So you aren't calling to see how I feel?" Katie asked.

"Oh, sure, yeah," Suzanne said. But she didn't sound very convincing. "I was going to ask how you were feeling *after* I told you about this really cool calendar my dad got for me."

"Oh," Katie said. "Well, I'm feeling better."

"I know, you just told me," Suzanne said. "So I don't have to ask. But aren't you going to ask *me* about my calendar?"

Katie sighed. A calendar didn't seem as important as being sick. But Suzanne obviously thought it was.

"What kind of calendar?" Katie asked her.

"It's pink with all kinds of glitter flowers and stickers on it," Suzanne said. "And there's a holiday on practically every day."

"A holiday every day?" Katie asked her.

"*Practically* every day," Suzanne corrected her. "Like tomorrow is Toothache Day."

"That doesn't sound like a very happy holiday," Katie said. "How do you celebrate Toothache Day?"

"Well, I'm going to call Dr. Sang, my dentist, and wish him a happy Toothache Day," Suzanne explained. "Toothache Day is great for dentists. It means more business for them."

Katie didn't think dentists actually wanted their patients to get toothaches. In fact, she was pretty sure they wanted people to brush and floss everyday so they *wouldn't* get them. But Katie didn't feel like arguing with Suzanne. She was getting a headache, and her throat hurt too much.

"Um, Suzanne, I'm kind of tired," Katie said. "I think I want to take a nap."

"Good idea," Suzanne agreed. "You want to rest up and feel better for Monday."

"Yes. I hate missing school," Katie said to her.

"No. I wasn't talking about school. Monday is Umbrella Day," Suzanne replied.

Katie sighed. "I sure don't want to miss an important holiday like that," she teased.

But Suzanne didn't hear the teasing tone in Katie's voice.

"I know," Suzanne agreed. "It's going to be so much fun!"

Chapter 3

Monday was a bright, sunny day. So a lot of kids were really surprised when Suzanne showed up on the playground with an open umbrella. But Katie wasn't surprised at all. She knew Suzanne would celebrate Umbrella Day, rain or shine.

"Nice umbrella." Katie complimented her friend as she looked at the yellow, green, and pink-striped umbrella Suzanne was carrying.

"Thanks," Suzanne replied. "It's my mom's favorite. But I didn't think she'd mind if I borrowed it for such an important holiday."

"What holiday?" Miriam Chan asked.

"Umbrella Day," Suzanne told her.

"That's not a real holiday," George Brennan insisted.

"Sure it is," Suzanne said. She reached into her backpack and pulled out her new calendar. "See, it says so right here!"

The kids all looked over Suzanne's shoulder. Sure enough, it said "Umbrella Day" in little red letters.

"Do you guys know what can go up a chimney down, but can't go down a chimney up?" George asked the other kids suddenly.

They all stared at him. What a weird question.

"An umbrella," George said, answering his own riddle. Then he started laughing.

It took Katie a minute, but then she got the joke. "That's a really good one, George."

"Thanks, Katie Kazoo," George replied, using the way-cool nickname he'd given her in third grade.

"Umbrella Day is nothing to laugh at," Suzanne insisted. "It's a very important holiday.

The rest of you should be celebrating with me."

★ ★ ★

Suzanne may have been celebrating Umbrella Day, but in Katie's class, the big celebration was for Presidents' Day. Mr. G. had gone wild decorating the classroom. There were flags; red, white, and blue streamers; and pictures of United States presidents everywhere. And the kids had all decorated their beanbag chairs for the holiday, too.

Emma W. had taped a picture of Thomas Jefferson and a copy of the Declaration of Independence to her chair.

Andy Epstein had used construction paper and cut-out stars to turn his beanbag into an American flag.

Kevin Camilleri had built a nest of pipe cleaners, and put a picture of an American eagle in it.

Mandy Banks decorated her beanbag chair with a big picture of the White House.

Katie's beanbag looked like a big, green

frog. She'd decorated it that way last week, when they were studying amphibian animals.

"Mr. G., can I still decorate my beanbag for Presidents' Day?" Katie asked her teacher.

"Sure you can," Mr. G. told her. "And while you're doing that, I'm going to tell the class about the great field trip we're all going on this Thursday."

The kids got very excited.

"A field trip!" George exclaimed. "How awesome is that?!"

"*Really* awesome," Kadeem Carter agreed. "Remember the field trip to the aquarium?"

Katie sighed. How could she forget? The magic wind had come right in the middle of the trip, and turned her into a fish! But of course Katie didn't say that. She just kept her mouth shut and concentrated on decorating her beanbag.

In the back of the room, Katie searched through the decorations in a big carton. She didn't see any pictures of Millard Fillmore.

Finally, Katie pulled out a funny picture of a man with a white beard and a red, white, and blue top hat. George leaned over and whispered, "That's Uncle Sam. We learned about him yesterday." Katie wasn't sure who Uncle Sam was. Still this looked like something good for Presidents' Day. So she taped it to her beanbag chair.

"Where are we going on this field trip?" Emma Stavros asked Mr. G.

"The Cherrydale Arena," Mr. G. told her. "We're going to see a very special show about America's presidents."

"Oh, I saw a commercial for that on TV," Mandy Banks said. "There's all kinds of singing and dancing."

"And they have actors playing the

presidents," Andy added.

"I want you dudes to know a lot about the presidents before we see the shows," Mr. G. said. "So on Wednesday, you'll each do an oral report on the president you're studying."

"Can we dress up like our president?" George asked. "I want to wear a white wig, like George Washington did."

"That's a great idea, George," Mr. G. said. "Anyone who wants to dress up as their president can definitely do that."

Mandy said, "I can wear a beard and a top hat like Abraham Lincoln."

Katie frowned. Mandy was lucky. It would be easy for her to dress like Abraham Lincoln. How was Katie supposed to dress up like Millard Fillmore? She had no idea what he looked like! And she had only two days to learn about him.

Chapter 4

Katie was very quiet while class 4A walked down the hall to the library later that day. Her head was hurting a little again. And she wasn't really looking forward to reading about Millard Fillmore, either.

"I liked the way you decorated your beanbag with the picture of Uncle Sam today," Mr. G. said as he walked beside Katie. "Do you know who he is?"

Katie shook her head. "I just liked the picture. Whose uncle is he?"

"Uncle Sam isn't a real person," Mr. G. explained to Katie. "He's a symbol—kind of like the eagle—for our government."

"Oh," Katie said. She got quiet again.
Then finally, she looked up at her teacher and
asked, "Mr. G., I have Millard Filmore and I
was wondering . . . Can I research a different
president?"

"Why, Katie?" Mr. G. asked.

"I want to learn about an *important*
president. One that really did something great,"
Katie told her teacher.

"I understand your point. But look at it this
way. In the whole history of our country, only
forty-four men have gotten to be president." Mr.
G. smiled. "Every one of them has tried his best
to help our country," he explained. "Some have
done more than others, but they have all tried
to make America a better place."

"Even Millard Fillmore?" Katie asked.

"Yep," Mr. G. said. "Wait until you read
about him. You'll see."

A few minutes later, Katie was sitting at a
desk in the library. Ms. Folio, the librarian,

had helped her find information about Millard Fillmore in a few books. Katie opened up one and began to read.

At first, Katie learned some not-so-interesting information, like the fact that Millard Fillmore was born in a log cabin in New York. When he grew up, he became a lawyer. And he was the thirteenth president.

Unfortunately, none of that was particularly fascinating. How was Katie ever going to find some way to give an interesting report on this guy?

Then, Katie read something that changed her mind about President Millard Fillmore. Something that really, *really* interested her:

Millard Fillmore was an animal lover. Although he did not bring any pets of his own to the White House, he started a chapter of the Society for the Prevention of Cruelty to Animals in Buffalo, New York. He also helped pass laws that made it illegal to hurt or injure animals.

"Wow!" Katie exclaimed happily. "Millard Fillmore and I have something in common."

"Shhh . . . You're in a library," Mr. G. whispered to Katie. But he wasn't angry. In fact, he was smiling.

"Maybe Millard Fillmore *was* a pretty good president," Katie whispered to her teacher.

"I'm sure the animals thought so," Mr. G. agreed.

Chapter 5

The next morning, when Katie arrived at school, the playground was almost empty. That wasn't very surprising. After all, it was pouring rain.

What *was* surprising was seeing Suzanne standing outside all by herself—without an umbrella. Instead, she was holding a ball of string and a pink and yellow plastic kite in her hands.

From under her umbrella, Katie asked her friend, "What are you doing?"

"I'm flying a kite," Suzanne said simply.

"Yes, I can see that. I meant, *why* are you out here in the rain flying a kite?" Katie explained. "Want to get under my umbrella?"

"No. It's Kite Day," Suzanne told Katie. "It's on my calendar."

Katie looked at Suzanne. She was sopping wet.

"You would have been better off if today was Umbrella Day," Katie told her.

Suzanne laughed. "But it's not. And I can't carry an umbrella and fly a kite at the same time. I love flying kites."

Katie watched Suzanne run across the wet playground, trying to get the kite to fly behind her. But the kite didn't take off. It just dragged along the ground behind her.

"I don't think it's windy enough for it to fly," Katie explained to Suzanne. Then she looked at the soaking wet kite, and her soaking wet friend. "Don't you want to come inside with me?"

Katie expected Suzanne to put up a fight and pretend she was having a great time.

Instead, Suzanne shrugged. "I guess so. I'm kind of done celebrating Kite Day."

The cafeteria was filled with wet kids. They were all waiting for it to be time to go to their classrooms. There were a few teachers in the cafeteria, too. It was their job to keep an eye on the kids.

"There's Mrs. Derkman," Suzanne told Katie. "You need to wave all your fingers at her."

"Why do I have to do that?" Katie asked.

"To celebrate Wave All Your Fingers at Your Neighbor Day," Suzanne told her.

"I thought you said today was Kite Day," Katie said.

"It is," Suzanne agreed. "But I got my calendar in the middle of the month. That means I missed a whole lot of holidays already. I'm trying to celebrate them, too."

"Then why don't *you* wave at Mrs. Derkman?" Katie asked her.

"Because she's not my neighbor. You're the one who lives next door to her," Suzanne explained.

It was hard for Katie to argue with that. Mrs. Derkman *was* her next-door neighbor. So Katie waved at the teacher with both of her hands.

Mrs. Derkman looked strangely at Katie. Then she shrugged and waved back at her.

"Why are you waving at Mrs. *Jerk*man?" George asked, as he and Kevin walked over to Katie and Suzanne.

Katie blushed. It was really embarrassing to be caught waving at a teacher. Especially a teacher who was as strict as Mrs. Derkman.

"Well . . . um . . . Suzanne wanted me to," Katie stammered. "She said . . ."

"Katie was just celebrating Wave All Your Fingers at Your Neighbor Day," Suzanne explained to George and Kevin.

"I never heard of that holiday," George told her.

"You haven't heard of a lot of things," Suzanne said.

"Why don't you celebrate Zip Your Lips,

Suzanne, Day?" George told her.

Kevin really cracked up at that one. "Zip Your Lips, Suzanne, Day," he repeated. "That's hilarious. Put that holiday in your calendar, Suzanne."

Suzanne rolled her eyes. "I'll have to check my calendar and see when Ignore Boys Day is," she told Katie. "That will really be something to celebrate!"

* * *

One thing was for sure . . . Suzanne definitely was not about to zip her lips.

At lunch that day, Suzanne sat down next to Jeremy Fox. Jeremy looked at Suzanne strangely. Katie was surprised, too. Usually Suzanne stayed as far from Jeremy as she could. But not today.

"Hi, Jeremy," Suzanne greeted him cheerfully. "How are you feeling? How are things going? Having a good day?"

"Um . . . okay, I guess," he answered suspiciously.

"Great," Suzanne said. "I'm doing very well today. Even though it's raining."

Jeremy shrugged. "Good," he answered.

"So, aren't you glad we're friends now?" Suzanne asked him.

"Huh?" Jeremy asked. He was totally confused.

"Since when are you two friends?" George asked Suzanne.

"I'm celebrating Make a Friend Day," Suzanne told him. "I picked Jeremy as my new friend."

"Well, pick someone else," Jeremy said.

George and Kevin both laughed.

"Speaking of celebrating," Mandy said, "I can't wait until tomorrow. That's when the kids in our class are giving our Presidents' Day oral reports."

"Yeah," George said. "My grandmother loaned me a wig, and I'm covering it with white powder. I'm also going to tuck my pants into knee socks, so they look like knickers. That's how men dressed in George Washington's time."

"Wait until you guys see how I look in my beard and top hat," Mandy told the others. "Guess what! A little girl wrote to Abraham Lincoln and said she thought he'd look good in a beard. So he grew one. I read that in this book I got."

"Katie, it's really too bad you didn't get Thomas Jefferson as your president," Emma W. said. "He had red hair just like you. I never knew that before. I also found out President Jefferson liked to play the violin. So Mr. Starkey is letting me borrow one from the music room for my presentation tomorrow."

Katie frowned. Her friends were all going to have such cool costumes and do cool things. Katie was just planning on wearing a tie, a jacket, and nice pants. That was how Millard Fillmore dressed. And from the pictures Katie had seen, he didn't even smile. That meant she was going to have to frown through her whole report.

Splash!

Just then, a carton of cold, wet milk flew across the table. It landed right in Katie's lap.

"Why did you do that?" Katie shouted. She

tried to mop up as much milk as she could with some paper napkins.

"Suzanne, you spilled that milk on purpose!" Mandy exclaimed.

"Yes, I know I did," Suzanne said with a smile. "I'm celebrating Don't Cry Over Spilled Milk Day."

"I can't believe you did that," Katie

exclaimed. She was definitely not smiling.

Lots of terrible things were happening. This morning, she'd embarrassed herself by waving at a teacher. She'd just found out her friends were all going to be wearing cooler costumes than she was. And now, her clothes all smelled like milk. *Yuck!*

This was just as bad as that day in third grade when she'd wished on that shooting star. Of course, Katie knew better than to wish again. But she could not stop a few tears from spilling.

"What are you doing?" Suzanne demanded. "It's Don't Cry Over Spilled Milk Day. Not Do Cry Over Spilled Milk Day. Look at me. *I'm* not crying."

"*You're* not covered in milk," Emma W. reminded her.

"I guess you're not going to be happy until March 9th," Suzanne told Katie.

Katie looked at her strangely. "What's so great about March 9th?" she asked.

"It's National *Get Over It* Day," Suzanne told her. "And that's exactly what you need to do. Get. Over. It."

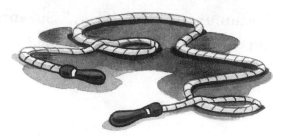

Chapter 6

Katie didn't wait until March to get over Suzanne and her silly holidays. By Wednesday morning, she was smiling again. It was hard not to be happy in class 4A. Especially today. All the kids were dressed in their costumes, getting ready for their Presidents' Day oral reports.

Katie had made herself a pretty decent costume. She didn't get to carry a violin like Emma W. or wear a beard and a top hat like Mandy, but she was dressed in one of her dad's dark blue suit jackets and a bow tie. She was also carrying a stack of books. She had written a very good report—she was sure no one else's would be like hers.

One by one, the kids began to make their speeches. Katie sat quietly in her beanbag chair waiting her turn. It wasn't easy to sit still. Katie was really excited to show Mr. G. and the class what she'd learned about Millard Fillmore.

"Okay," Mr. G. said. "We don't have much time left. But Katie Kazoo, you haven't gone yet. Are you ready to tell us all you know about President Fillmore?"

"I sure am!" Katie exclaimed. She leaped to her feet and walked toward the front of the room.

"Millard Fillmore wasn't elected president," she told the class. "He was the *vice* president. But when President Zachary Taylor suddenly got sick and died, he became the president."

Katie looked out at the class. They were starting to look a little bored. But Katie was ready for that. She smiled brightly at her friends. And then, she broke into a rap she had written especially for today.

She held up the stack of books. "Millard Fillmore loved to read, so lots of books he did need. In the White House there weren't any. So Millard F. donated many. He started a library right away, which presidents still use today."

Katie was really on a roll now. The kids in her class were clapping in time to her rap.

Katie went on. "Millard Fillmore is the one, who made sure all animals had fun. He founded a local ASPCA, where cats and dogs could safely play. Fillmore's not a president of fame, but he helped our country just the same."

Rrring. Just then the bell rang. It was time for lunch.

Katie frowned. "But I haven't finished my report," she told Mr. G.

"I'm sorry," Mr. G. said. "But time's up. Don't feel too badly, Katie. We all know a lot more about Millard Fillmore now. That was a really creative way to teach us."

Katie smiled brightly. She was proud that her teacher had liked her report. She'd actually had a lot of fun writing it.

As she walked down the hall to the cafeteria, she hummed to herself. "Fillmore's not a president of fame, but he helped our country just the same."

★ ★ ★

The kids in class 4A were all talking about

their oral reports during lunch.

"That was so much fun!" Emma S. said. "I loved when George's white wig fell off."

"I meant to do that," George told her. Katie giggled. She knew that wasn't true. George knew it, too. He laughed with her.

"Your rap was really cool, Katie," Emma W. told her.

"Yeah," Kevin agreed. "You found a really good way to make a boring president seem interesting."

"Actually Millard Fillmore wasn't so boring," Katie told him.

"Who's boring?" Suzanne asked, as she walked over to the table. "Not me. That's for sure."

Katie just looked at Suzanne but didn't say anything. She was still a little annoyed with her.

"Relax," Suzanne said. "I celebrated Don't Cry Over Spilled Milk Day yesterday."

Katie smiled and moved over to make room for Suzanne. "Then that means today is You Can

Sit Next to Me Day," she said.

Suzanne didn't mention a holiday during lunch. She just sat there, eating her lunch. Which was very strange behavior—at least for Suzanne.

"Why are you so quiet? Is today It's Nothing Special Day?" Emma W. finally asked Suzanne.

Suzanne shook her head and laughed. "That would be a very silly holiday."

Katie didn't think it was any sillier than Wave All Your Fingers at Your Neighbor Day, or Toothache Day.

"Today happens to be a very special day," Suzanne told the other fourth-graders. "But you will have to wait to find out what it is."

✦ ✦ ✦

Miriam, Zoe, and Mandy had already started a game of double Dutch jump rope by the time Katie and Suzanne got out onto the playground after lunch.

"Do you want to go over and jump rope with them?" Katie asked Suzanne.

Suzanne didn't answer. Instead, she held her finger in the air. "Hmmmm. The wind seems to be coming from the east at about ten miles an hour."

Katie looked curiously at Suzanne. "What are you talking about?" she asked.

"The wind," Suzanne explained. "I think that's the reason it feels colder than forty-eight degrees. The temperature was supposed to go that high today. Don't you think it feels chilly, Katie?"

"Um . . . I guess," Katie said. So what if it was a little chilly and windy? Just as long as it wasn't the magic wind, Katie didn't mind. "We won't feel cold once we're jumping rope."

Suzanne nodded slowly. "Well, at least it's partly sunny out. And although there are a few clouds in the sky, I don't predict any rain for today. In fact, I'd say there's no more than a 20 percent chance of rain."

"Fine. I'm glad to hear it. Look, Suzanne, do you or don't you want to go jump rope?" Katie asked. "Or are we going to talk about rain some more?"

"Katie, be serious," Suzanne said. "Today is an important holiday."

"What holiday is it?" Katie asked her.

Suzanne grinned widely as if she'd been waiting for Katie to ask that question. "It's National Weatherperson's Day."

Katie groaned. So that explained Suzanne's sudden fascination with the sun, the wind, and the temperature.

"Happy Weatherperson's Day," Katie said. "I'm going over to jump rope with Mandy, Miriam, and Zoe."

"But National Jump Rope Day isn't until October," Suzanne told her.

"Maybe not," Katie said. "But I've heard that when it's forty-eight degrees, and the wind is coming from the east, and there's just a slight chance of rain, it is the perfect time for jumping rope. See you later, Suzanne."

Chapter 7

"George, stop kicking my seat!" Suzanne exclaimed angrily.

It was Thursday morning. The Cherrydale Elementary School fourth-graders were all seated in the audience of the Cherrydale Arena waiting for the Presidents' Day show to begin.

The kids were very excited. They could barely sit still. Especially George. He had trouble sitting still even when he wasn't on a field trip.

"I didn't kick your seat, Suzanne," George insisted. "It was Kevin."

"Blame Someone Else Day isn't until May,"

Suzanne told him. "This is February."

"We're supposed to be here celebrating *Presidents' Day*," Katie reminded her friends. "Mr. G. told us he wanted us to behave during the show."

"Exactly," Suzanne told George and Kevin. "We're not the only people at the Cherrydale Arena today. Other people came here to enjoy the show, too."

"Ms. Sweet made our class promise to behave, too," Becky Stern said. "Isn't that right, Jeremy?"

Jeremy just shrugged. Katie had a feeling the last thing he wanted to do was talk to Becky. She had a big crush on Jeremy. But Jeremy did not have a crush on her.

"The show doesn't start for five more minutes," George insisted. "We'll be quiet then."

Katie nodded and got up from her seat. "Excuse me, Suzanne," she said as she crawled over her friend's legs and into the aisle.

"Where are you going?" Suzanne asked her.

"To the bathroom," Katie whispered. "My mother has been making me drink gallons of orange juice so I don't get another cold. I'm in the bathroom a lot."

"Well, hurry back," Suzanne told her. "The show's going to start any minute."

"Yeah, hurry up, Katie Kazoo," Kevin said. "You don't want to miss the Parade of Presidents."

Katie nodded. "I'll be back in a sec," she assured her friends.

Unfortunately, there was a line for the bathroom when Katie got there. She just had to stand there and wait . . . and wait . . . and wait. Soon, she could hear music starting inside the theater.

Finally, it was her turn. She went in a stall and shut the door. And then she felt a cool breeze blowing on the back of her neck.

That was strange. There weren't any windows in the bathroom. And the door was shut tight. Where was that breeze coming from?

Before Katie could take another look around, the cool breeze picked up speed, becoming a cold wind. *A wind that was circling just around Katie.* Oh no! This wasn't just any wind. This was the magic wind!

"Not now!" Katie shouted out. "I've been waiting all week to see this show. Go away, magic wind!"

But the magic wind didn't listen to Katie. Instead it grew stronger and stronger, circling around her like a wild tornado. Katie shut her eyes tight and tried really hard not to cry.

And then it stopped. Just like that. The magic wind was gone.

And so was Katie Carew. She'd turned into someone else. One . . . two . . . switcheroo! But who?

Chapter 8

Katie opened her eyes and looked around. That was strange. She was suddenly in the back of the theater, behind the last row of seats. At least that's where she thought she was. It was so dark, it was hard to tell.

Gak. Katie felt a strange choking feeling around her neck. She reached up, and loosened her tie a little. *Ahh.* That was better.

Wait a minute. *Her tie?* Katie wasn't wearing a tie today. She was wearing her new blue denim dress. Or at least that's what she'd been wearing before the magic wind had arrived.

Katie looked down at her feet. Her bright

red high-top sneakers were gone. Instead she was wearing a pair of dancing shoes. *Men's* dancing shoes.

That could only mean one thing. The magic wind had turned Katie into a man. But *which* man?

Just then, a guy with a clipboard came over to talk to Katie. "Now remember, you follow Zachary Taylor in the Parade of Presidents," he told her. "We're doing this in order."

Katie looked at the guy strangely. "Who are you?" she asked him.

"What are you talking about?" the man wondered. "I'm Sam, the stage manager. Quit clowning around. The show starts in one minute."

Katie gasped. If Sam was the stage manager, that must mean that Katie had been switcherooed into one of the actors. And not just any actor. Katie thought for a moment. She was supposed to follow Zachary Taylor in the parade. So she must be the actor playing the president who came right after Taylor . . . and that was none other than Millard Fillmore!

The show was starting in just one minute! Katie didn't know any of the songs or lines Millard Fillmore was supposed to say. She had to get out of this.

"Sam, I can't go on," she told the stage manager. "I'm too nervous. I don't remember any of my lines."

Sam sighed. "Stop cracking jokes," he told Katie. "You're Millard Fillmore. You don't have any lines. Only the really famous presidents have lines."

And with that, the music started. It was time for the show to begin. There was no way Katie was getting out of this now.

She took a deep breath. *Come on. You can do it*, she told herself. *Just follow the other actors. You don't have to say anything.*

In the distance, Katie could hear the orchestra playing. It was that song they played whenever the president walked into a room.

She'd heard it on TV. It was called "Hail to the Chief."

One by one, the actors playing the presidents began to parade down the aisle of the Cherrydale Arena—and that included Katie.

It didn't take long for all the actors to reach the stage. Katie stood there in her place, right between Zachary Taylor and Franklin Pierce.

This isn't so bad, she thought to herself. *I'll just stand here and keep quiet.*

But it wasn't going to be that easy. At just that moment, a new song started. And the actors all began to do a dance.

Katie tried to follow, but it was hard. She turned right, when the others turned left. She raised her hands, when the others spread them wide apart.

It's a good thing I'm not in the front row, Katie thought to herself. *Maybe no one can see me.*

The audience might not have been able to see her, but the other dancers sure could.

"What is wrong with you, Phil?" the actor playing Franklin Pierce hissed at her. "Get it together, will ya?"

"I'm trying," Katie told him. She sounded more like a scared fourth-grade girl than a grown man.

Just then, the man playing George Washington took his place in the spotlight. He smiled at the audience, and began to sing a solo.

Whew! Katie was off the hook—at least for a little while.

"I'm the father of our country, George Washington. When it comes to fighting for liberty, I'm the one. I led our forces against the British. Although my men weren't trained and our horses were skittish. And when at last the war was done, I became president number one."

As the audience cheered for George Washington, the music started up. Once again, the presidents began a dance routine. Katie struggled to keep up, but she was always a few steps behind. And it only got worse when the presidents linked arms, two by two, and began to whirl each other around. Katie grabbed the Franklin Pierce actor's hand. She kicked out with her left foot and let her free arm fly out to her side like an airplane wing.

Katie was trying her best to copy what everyone else was doing. With any luck, the dance routine would end soon. Then suddenly she felt her free hand hit something . . .

Actually, her hand had hit *somebody*!

She turned around. Oh no! She'd punched the Abraham Lincoln actor in the face. He stood there in his beard with his nose bleeding all over the place.

"Ouch!" he cried. He held a hankie over his nose. "I'm supposed to speak next. I can't."

He sounded just like Katie did when she had a cold.

"I'm so sor—" she whispered. Then she felt a hot light beaming on her face.

The music kept playing. Abraham Lincoln

kept bleeding. And the crowd kept staring at
the stage, waiting for something to happen.

"Sing something . . ." the Zachary Taylor
actor whispered to her. "Anything."

Katie froze with fear. This was *soooo* not
good.

Chapter 9

Katie stood onstage staring at all the people staring at her. She could see George and Suzanne and Mr. G. in the audience. Then, suddenly, Katie got one of her great ideas! There *was* a presidential song she knew. It was about Millard Fillmore. She'd written it for her class.

Katie smiled brightly. She opened her mouth to sing.

And then she stopped. Maybe that wasn't such a good idea after all. Katie *couldn't* sing the Millard Fillmore song that her class had already heard. They would wonder how the actor onstage knew Katie's song.

There were the other verses to her Millard Fillmore rap. The ones she hadn't had time to read to her class. If Katie could just sing those words instead of rapping them, then . . .

Katie cleared her throat and began. "I'm the thirteenth president, Millard Fillmore. My mama and daddy were very poor. But I studied law and got real smart, til in politics I got my start. Then one day I became president, and to the White House I was sent. President's a job with no rest, but I promise that I did my best. I had a really great foreign plan, and I started our friendship with Japan. I really did try very hard. Think of that when you hear Millard."

As Katie finished the last note of her song, the other presidents started dancing again. After all, the show had to go on.

But not for Katie. She'd had enough of being in the spotlight. So as soon as no one was looking, Katie danced her way off the stage.

"Hey, where are you going?" Sam the stage manager asked.

Katie didn't answer. She just ran offstage and down a dark hallway. She stopped for a moment to catch her breath. She was glad to be alone. Had she really just sung in front of the entire audience in the Cherrydale Arena?

It was awfully cold in the hallway. And a little windy. Katie could feel a cool breeze blowing on the back of her neck.

In seconds, the breeze picked up speed. Before Katie knew what was happening, that gentle breeze became a wild tornado. A tornado that was circling only around Katie.

That could only mean one thing. The magic wind was back. And it was stronger than ever!

The magic wind blew harder and harder. It was whirling and swirling so powerfully that Katie was sure she was going to blown away.

And then it stopped. Just like that.

The magic wind was gone. Katie Carew was back!

And so was the actor who was playing Millard Fillmore. In fact, he was standing right beside Katie in the hallway. And boy, was he confused!

"What am I doing backstage?" he asked Katie. "What are *you* doing backstage? And *who* are you?"

"I'm Katie Carew," Katie answered. She figured that was the easiest question to answer. "I'm here with kids from my school."

"I'm Phil Stanza," Phil said. "I play Millard Fillmore in the show."

"I know," Katie said. "You're dressed just like him."

"But why aren't I onstage?" Phil asked Katie.

"Well, I . . I mean, *you* sang your song, and you left . . ." Katie began. "I mean you *exited*," Katie said, using the theater word.

Phil looked at her strangely. "I sang?" he asked her. "I'm not supposed to do that."

"You were really good," she assured him. "Everyone clapped."

Phil shook his head. "Man, the director is going to be so mad. I wasn't supposed to have any lines or solos in this thing. But I kind of remember singing something about Japan, I think."

"You did," Katie told him.

Phil shook his head. "I'll be lucky if I don't get fired!" he exclaimed.

"Fired?" Katie asked nervously. "But, you jumped right in. You sang a song. Everyone liked you."

"I don't know about that," Phil said sadly. "But I do know I'd better get back onstage for the finale. And you'd better get back to your seat. Your teacher will be wondering where you went."

Phil was right. Mr. G. was probably already a little worried about her.

"Okay. Well, good . . ." Katie stopped herself. She knew you weren't supposed to tell actors good luck before a show. That was bad luck. And after what happened in the show, Phil was going to need all the good luck he could find.

So all Katie said was, "Good-*bye*."

Chapter 10

"Where have you been?" Suzanne whispered as Katie sat down in her seat. "You missed the whole Parade of Presidents."

"There, um, well, there was a long line at the bathroom," Katie whispered back.

"Your president, Millard Fillmore, sang a funny song," Andy told her. "Too bad you missed it."

Katie smiled. She hadn't missed it at all. But of course she didn't tell Suzanne and Andy that.

"Shhh . . ." Mandy whispered to the girls. "Abraham Lincoln is making a speech."

Katie looked up at the stage. Sure enough,

the actor playing President Lincoln was in the spotlight. His nose wasn't bleeding anymore.

"Four score and seven years ago," he began, "our fathers brought forth, upon this continent, a new nation . . ."

Katie sat up tall. For a few minutes, she had been president of the United States. At least, in the Cherrydale Arena. And that was something to be proud of.

★ ★ ★

When the show was over, the fourth grade left the theater. The kids were still really excited.

"That was pretty awesome!" Kevin exclaimed. "Franklin Delano Roosevelt looked exactly like he did in the pictures in the books I read."

"The actors' costumes were definitely better than ours were," Emma W. said.

"Yeah, at least their wigs stayed on," Kadeem joked. He pointed to George and laughed.

"I told you guys, I made my wig fall off on purpose," George insisted. "I was just being funny."

"Yeah right," Kadeem said.

"Hey, look!" Suzanne exclaimed suddenly. "A reporter is talking into a camera over there." She grabbed Katie by the arm. "Let's go stand behind her and be on TV!"

Before Katie knew what was happening, Suzanne had dragged her over to where the cameraman and news reporter were standing. Suzanne waved her arms up and down and smiled. Katie just stood there, looking embarrassed.

"I'm here at the Cherrydale Arena, where the Presidents' Day Extravaganza has just finished its first performance," the reporter said into her microphone. "And while there were many wonderful moments in this show, there was one problem. There was a collision, and the actor playing Millard Fillmore suddenly found himself center stage. It was definitely strange. Especially since he's a president nobody cares about."

Katie couldn't believe her ears. The reporter

was being so mean. And that made Katie mad. *Really* mad!

"I care about him!" Katie blurted out suddenly. "And he cared about America!"

The reporter stopped and turned around. "Excuse me?" she asked.

Oops. Katie blushed. "I . . . um . . . well, I just meant Millard Fillmore tried really hard. I studied him for school. He started a library in the White House, and he helped animals, and he made friends with Japan . . ."

The reporter sighed. "Are you saying you thought that the mess up in today's show that forced Millard Fillmore front and center made the show *better*?"

Katie frowned. That wasn't what she'd been saying, exactly. Just then, Katie remembered something Mr. G. had said.

"In the whole history of our country, only forty-four people have been president," Katie said. "All of them have tried to make the US a better place. Even the ones who aren't so popular."

The reporter stared at Katie for a minute. Then she looked back into the camera. "You know, you're a very smart girl," the reporter said.

Katie smiled proudly into the camera.

"I take it back, folks," the reporter said. "Millard Fillmore actually helped make the show extra special."

Katie smiled. Hooray! Phil was a star. And so was Millard Fillmore.

Chapter 11

Ring. Ring. Katie's phone rang early on Saturday morning.

"Hello?" Katie said.

"Hi, Katie, it's me," Suzanne said. "I called to find out what you're doing today."

"I'm going to the mall with my mom," Katie said. "She has to work at the bookstore."

"That's perfect!" Suzanne exclaimed.

"What is?" Katie asked.

"You going to the mall," Suzanne explained. "That's the perfect place to celebrate."

Katie sighed. "Suzanne, I don't really want to celebrate any weird holidays today," she said.

"Oh, this holiday isn't weird," Suzanne

assured her. "In fact, you're going to love it."

"Which holiday is it?" Katie asked.

But Suzanne wasn't telling. "Just meet me at the fountain at eleven o'clock," she said.

✴ ✴ ✴

Katie checked the big clock as she walked toward the fountain in the middle of the Cherrydale Mall later that morning. It was just before eleven. She had no idea what Suzanne wanted to celebrate. She just hoped it wasn't anything too embarrassing.

A minute later, Suzanne arrived. She looked pretty normal. Katie breathed a sigh of relief. At least it wasn't Weird Hat Day or Big Red Clown Nose Day or anything.

"Are you ready?" Suzanne asked excitedly as Katie came over to her.

"For what?" Katie asked.

Suzanne pointed to Cinnamon's Candy Shop. "For that!" she shouted excitedly.

Katie looked over at the store. There was a big sign in the window. It said:

Happy Gumdrop Day!

"Gumdrop Day?" Katie asked excitedly.

Suzanne nodded. "Cinnamon's giving out free gumdrops all day long!"

"Well, what are we waiting for?" Katie asked.

"Hi, there," Cinnamon greeted the girls as they came in the front door. "Happy Gumdrop Day!"

"Happy Gumdrop Day to you, too!" Katie replied.

"Where are the free gumdrops?" Suzanne asked excitedly.

Cinnamon pointed to a big, plastic barrel filled with colorful candies. "Right there," she told Suzanne. "Help yourself."

"All right!" Suzanne said. She raced over and scooped a bunch of gumdrops into a bag with a plastic shovel.

Katie followed and filled a small bag of gumdrops, too. *Mmmm.* They were delicious.

"Now aren't you glad I have my calendar, Katie?" she asked. "I called Cinnamon when I

saw what day it is. And right away she said she was going to give away free gumdrops."

"I'm just glad it wasn't Garlic Day," Katie teased.

Suzanne made a face. "I know what you mean," she said.

"You mean there actually is a Garlic Day?"

"Oh yes. There's Hooray for Turnips Day, too. And believe me, I don't like eating garlic or turnips. But I guess I'll have to when those holidays come around."

Katie giggled. No matter how crazy she got, Suzanne was always fun to be around.

"Don't ever change, Suzanne," Katie told her best friend.

"I won't," Suzanne assured her. "And don't you ever change, either. Okay, Katie?"

Katie didn't answer. Instead, she popped another gumdrop in her mouth. After all, that was one promise she couldn't make. At least not as long as the magic wind was still around.

George Brown, CLASS CLOWN

Here is the first chapter of the
first book in a brand-new series that
stars Katie Kazoo's pal George.

Chapter 1

Yo, George,

Never thought I'd say this, but I think it stinks that you won't be going to our school anymore. Now I'll be the only one in class 4A telling jokes, and my jokes always sounded better next to yours.

At least at your new school, you can be the funny guy.

Your pal,
Kadeem

George lay on his bed and stared at Kadeem's page in the Good-bye Book the kids at his old school had made for him. All the fourth-graders had written something. But Kadeem's was the one that made George the saddest and the maddest. Sad because now he had no friends to tell jokes to. And mad because Kadeem made it sound like his jokes were funnier than George's. And that wasn't true. No way!

George reread what Kevin, his best friend, had written. At least Kevin *used* to be George's best friend. It was pretty hard to stay best friends with someone who lived far away.

George,

I was just thinking about the time in third grade when you put the fake spider on Mrs. Derkman's chair in the cafeteria. I never heard anyone scream so loud. I laughed so hard, milk came out of my nose.

Boy, will I miss you,
Kevin

George started to laugh. That *had* been a good one. No one was more afraid of bugs than mean Mrs. *Jerk*man. (That was what George had always called his strict third-grade teacher—at least behind her back.) Freaking her out was always fun.

George turned the page in his Good-bye Book. The next note was from Suzanne Lock.

George,

> *Good-bye.*

> *Suzanne*

That cheered George up. He thought it was really, really funny. Suzanne hadn't wanted to write in his Good-bye Book. Her teacher had made her do it. Not that George blamed Suzanne. It wasn't like they'd ever been friends or anything.

But the note on the page next to Suzanne's was from one of George's really good friends.

Dear George,

> *I'm really going to miss you. You made me laugh—a lot. I think you are really*

brave. I'd be scared to move to a new town.
But you don't seem scared at all. I know you
will have a lot of friends in Beaver Brook.
    Your friend,
    Katie Kazoo
    PS—Thanks for the way-cool nickname.

George remembered how he had given Katie
that name. He'd decided that her last name,
Carew, sounded like a kazoo. And the name had
stuck.

Katie was a really good friend. And she was
pretty smart. But she was also really wrong
about George. He *was* scared to be living in a
new town and starting at a new school today.

George had a lot of practice being the new
kid. His dad was in the army and his family
moved around a lot. But it was never easy. After
spending two whole years in Cherrydale, he had
almost started feeling like an "old" kid. Then—
BAM—here he was in Beaver Brook.

"George! It's 0-800 hours. Gotta get a move on!
Front and center!"

His dad's deep voice echoed through the halls of their new house. It was a lot bigger than their old house. Even with all their furniture, it felt empty. In fact, the long upstairs hallway would be great for skateboarding— except his mom never let him skateboard in the house.

George grabbed his backpack and headed downstairs. For a second, he thought about sliding down the banister. Then he stopped himself. That was something the *old* George would do. Now, besides being the new kid, he wanted to be a new George. And the new George didn't do dumb stuff like that—dumb stuff that got him into trouble.

The last time George slid down a banister was at his old school. He'd flipped over the side of the staircase and wound up with a black eye and a bloody nose. And not just a regular bloody nose. A supercolossal bloody nose. The kind that turns your nose into a blood fountain. The school nurse said she'd never seen anything like it. It had been sort of gross. But sort of cool, too.

"Got everything, honey?" George's mom asked as he reached the bottom of the stairs. "Pencils? Notebooks? Lunch?"

"Check, check, and check," George said.

"That shirt looks really nice on you," his mother told him.

George looked down at his new green T-shirt. It had a picture of a guy on a skateboard flying right across the middle of it. It was really cool. The perfect first day of school shirt.

"Thanks," George told his mom.

"Okay, soldier," his dad said. "Ready to march?"

"Yes, sir," George answered. He saluted his dad. His dad saluted back and then gave him a big bear hug.

"Then let's go," George's dad said.

As George headed to his new school, he thought about Cherrydale Elementary School.

Not to brag, but everybody there liked him. He was famous for being the funny kid—the class clown. Of course, pranks also got him into more trouble than anyone else. It seemed to George that he'd spent as much time in the principal's office as in class.

But that wasn't going to happen in Beaver Brook. No more class clown! George was turning over a new leaf. He was through with getting in trouble. He was going to act differently from now on. *So* differently, in fact, that he'd decided to start school with a new last name. His dad's last name was Brennan. And that was the last name George had used all his life. There was nothing wrong with that name. But from now on, George was using his mom's last name: Brown. New name, new George.

"George Brown," George murmured quietly under his breath. "George Brown."

"What did you say?" his dad asked him.

"I was just trying out my new name," George explained.

"Oh," George's dad replied.

"You're okay about this, aren't you, Dad?" George asked his father.

"Sure." Only his dad didn't sound so sure. "I guess it'll just take a little getting used to. But I understand wanting to change things up. Look at me. I've traveled all over with the army. New people, new cities. Lots of changes."

That was true. His dad's job was the reason the family was always moving. It was why George always seemed to be the new kid.

"But we're going to stay at this base for a while," George's dad continued. "At least I hope so. Your mom is really excited to have opened her own store here in Beaver Brook. I don't think she wants to pack up and move again."

"Yeah, I guess," George said. Having a dad in the army was cool. But having a mom who owned the Knit Wit Craft Shop—a store that sold yarn, knitting needles, and beads—was, well . . . not so much.

George kept up with his dad's long strides,

trying to ignore the nervous feeling in his stomach. His mom called it having butterflies in your belly. But that wasn't what it felt like. It was more like worms. Big, long, slimy, nervous worms slithering around inside.

They turned a corner. There it was. George stopped and stared at his new school. It was a red-brick building with a flagpole in front. Over the door it said EDITH B. SUGARMAN ELEMENTARY SCHOOL. Except for the name, it looked pretty much like all the other schools George had gone to.

"Edith B. Sugarman?" George wondered. "Is that somebody famous?"

His dad shrugged. "Never heard of her. But the name doesn't really matter. Your new school has a fine reputation."

George didn't agree at all. Names did matter. A lot. And no one knew that better than *George Brown*.